THE BEAR & THE FLY

a story by
PAULA WINTER

Crown Publishers, Inc.   New York

Manufactured in Italy
Published simultaneously in Canada
by General Publishing Company Limited
10 9 8 7 6 5 4

The illustrations are black ink drawings
with pencil shaded overlays prepared by the
artist and printed in three colors.

Library of Congress Cataloging in Publication Data
Winter, Paula.
The bear and the fly.
Summary: A bear tries to catch a fly with
disastrous results.
[1. Bears—Fiction. 2. Stories without
words] I. Title.
PZ7.W762Be   [E]   76-2479
ISBN 0-517-52605-0

For Norma Jean